Gobbo

HarperCollins *Children's Books*

It was a cloudy day in Toyland and the Goblins were bored. Everybody in Toy Town was busy at work and none of the Goblins' usual tricks were working.

In fact, nothing was going right for the sneaky pair.

Earlier that morning,
Gobbo had tried to steal a big plate of
googleberry muffins from
Master Tubby Bear.

But he had left a long trail of crumbs behind
him and Mr Plod had given him a good
telling off!

Then Sly had tried to mix up Big-Ears'
washing with Miss Pink Cat's.

But even that hadn't worked.

Miss Pink Cat had heard Sly
creeping around and sloshed
a strawberry ice-cream on
top of his head!

Meanwhile, Noddy was having a very busy day. He had been whizzing around Toy Town all morning taking his friends from place to place in his shiny little taxi.

"Parp! Parp!"

Noddy waved as he sped past the sulking Goblins on his way to pick up his friends.

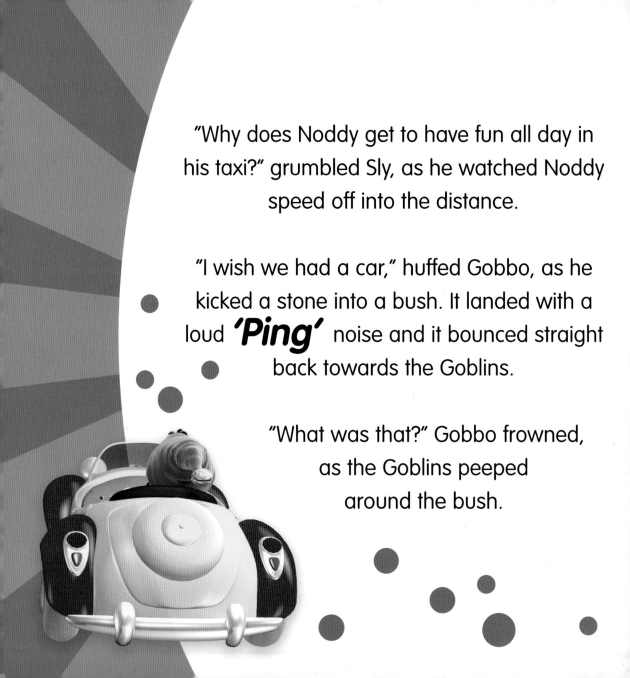

"Why does Noddy get to have fun all day in his taxi?" grumbled Sly, as he watched Noddy speed off into the distance.

"I wish we had a car," huffed Gobbo, as he kicked a stone into a bush. It landed with a loud **'Ping'** noise and it bounced straight back towards the Goblins.

"What was that?" Gobbo frowned, as the Goblins peeped around the bush.

There, lying in the middle of the bush was an old, rusty rickshaw. Gobbo went to grab the bike when Big-Ears suddenly appeared.

"Have you Goblins seen my old rickshaw anywhere?" Big-Ears asked, suspiciously.

"Well, we've just found. . ." Sly started. "Nothing!" Gobbo interrupted, glaring at Sly. "We don't know anything. Not us!"

"Well, if you do see it,"
Big-Ears began,
looking worried.
"Let me know. It is **very**
important that I get it back."

"Of course!" replied Sly, smirking.
"You can always count on us,"
sneered Gobbo,
hiding the rickshaw.

As soon as Big-Ears was out of sight, Gobbo pulled the rickshaw out of the bush and dusted off the branches.

"Look at this, Sly!" Gobbo cried, as they jumped on and tried to pedal.

Before they could say **'Go!'** they were speeding around the square. They went so fast, they almost bumped right into Mr Plod!

"Hey!" Mr Plod cried, blowing his whistle. "Watch out, you naughty Goblins!"

But Gobbo didn't care. Now he had
a vehicle of his very own!

Then they saw Mrs Skittle.
She had been shopping all morning and
was over the moon when the Goblins
stopped to give her a lift.

"Welcome to Racing Rickshaws!"
chortled Gobbo.

"The fastest bike in the whole of Toy Town!"
chirped Sly, as the rusty rickshaw lurched
into action once more.

This time when Gobbo tried to pedal, the rickshaw started bouncing up and down and spinning around and around. Gobbo tried to control it but the rickshaw jiggled around so much they all nearly fell out!

Mrs Skittle's shopping flew out of the car and started rolling down the street.

Mrs Skittle jumped out as fast as she could. "You silly Goblins! I feel very dizzy now!" she cried, as she started to pick up all of her shopping.

Meanwhile, over at Toadstool House, Big-Ears was telling Noddy about his strange morning.

"I was fixing my rickshaw with some magic powder," began Big-Ears, looking worried. "But I think I may have used the wrong magic."

"What do you mean?" asked Noddy.

"Well, it started spluttering and spinning around and around, smashing all my glasses and then it shot right out of the door!" he cried. "I just hope nobody is using it. Who knows where it would take them?"

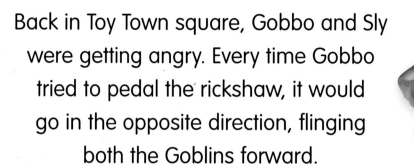

Back in Toy Town square, Gobbo and Sly were getting angry. Every time Gobbo tried to pedal the rickshaw, it would go in the opposite direction, flinging both the Goblins forward.

"You silly old rickshaw!" Gobbo shouted. "You are no good to anybody!"

Suddenly, the rickshaw leaped forward with such force that the Goblins flew right out onto the road!

"Crash!"

The Goblins crashed straight into a brick wall!

Big-Ears and Noddy had arrived and ran
over to the Goblins, lying on the floor.

"Stay away from that rickshaw!"
Big-Ears called out to the Goblins.
"It is in a most troublesome mood!"

But before Big-Ears could say anything else,
Gobbo jumped back into the rickshaw.

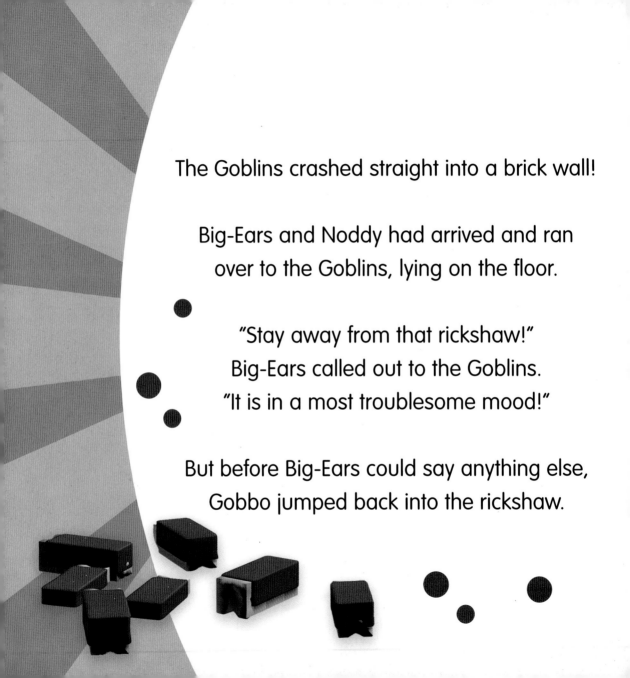

Then, without warning, the rickshaw started to splutter and groan and Gobbo went hurtling up into the sky!

"Whoa! What's happening?" cried poor Gobbo, as he whizzed above Toy Town.

"This naughty rickshaw is making spells without me!" said Big-Ears.

Big-Ears thought quickly and sprinkled some special magic dust onto the naughty rickshaw.

Gobbo suddenly came shooting down
from the sky and landed with a bang,
right on top of Sly!

"Hey!" Sly shouted and shoved
Gobbo off him.

"That will teach you to play with things that
aren't yours, Gobbo," Big-Ears warned,
as he pulled the Goblins to their feet.

"For once," Gobbo began, as he
brushed the rubble from his jacket,
"I have agree with you!"

First published in the UK by HarperCollins Children's Books in 2008

1 3 5 7 9 10 8 6 4 2
ISBN-13: 978-0-00-726925-9
ISBN-10: 0-00-726925-0

Printed and bound in China

NODDY™

Star in your very own PERSONALISED Noddy book!

In just 3 easy steps your child can join Noddy in a Toyland adventure!

1 Go to www.MyNoddyBook.co.uk

2 Personalise your book

3 Checkout!

3 Great Noddy adventures to choose from:

'Your child' Saves Toytown

Soar through a rainbow in Noddy's aeroplane to help him save Toytown.

A Gift for 'your child'

Noddy composes a song for your child in this story for a special occasion.

A Christmas Gift for 'your child'

Noddy composes a song for your child in a Christmas version of the above story.

Visit today to find out more and create your personalised Noddy book!

www.MyNODDYBook.co.uk